This Little Tiger book
belongs to:

_____

_____

For my little family –
every day, now and always, all my love. XO!
– N B

With love to Louise and Eloise
– J L

LITTLE TIGER PRESS
I The Coda Centre, 189 Munster Road,
London SW6 6AW

First published in Great Britain 2016
This edition published 2016
Text copyright © Nicky Benson 2016
Illustrations copyright © Jonny Lambert 2016

A CIP catalogue record for this book is available from
the British Library
All rights reserved • ISBN 978-1-84869-199-5

Printed in China • LTP/1800/1383/1015

2 4 6 8 10 9 7 5 3 1

I love you
more
and more

Nicky Benson

Jonny Lambert

LITTLE TIGER PRESS
London

You are my everything,
I love you high and low.

I love you more than flowers
love to blossom, bloom and grow.

I love you more than trees
love to change with every season.

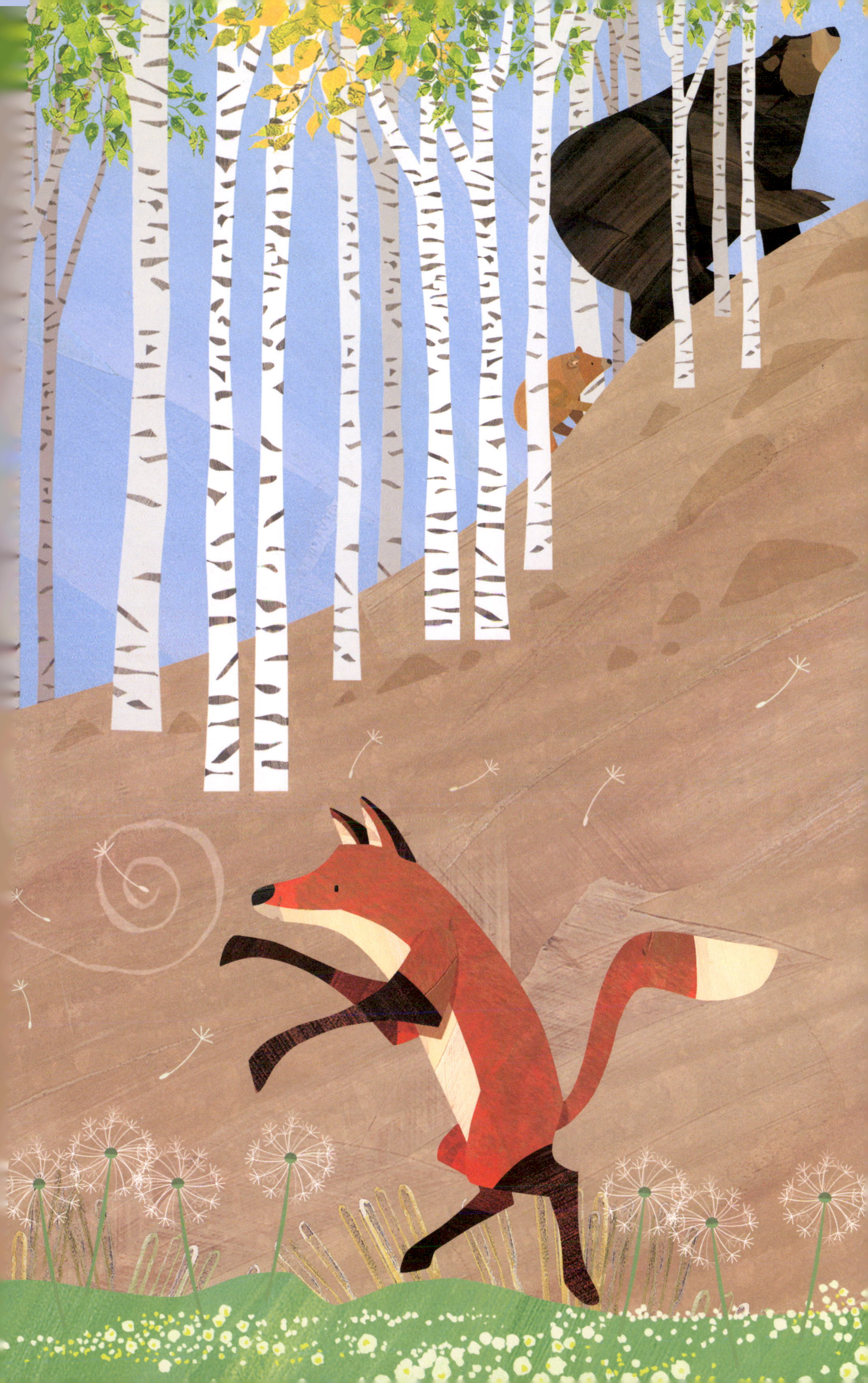

I love you more than anything,
I cannot name just one reason.

I love you more than waterfalls
love to splash on me and you.

I love you more than fish
love to swim in rivers blue.

I love you more than mountains
love the clouds breezing by.

I love you more than stars
love to sparkle in the sky.

You are beautiful in all you do,
and in all the words you say . . .

I love you, baby, more and more
with every precious day.

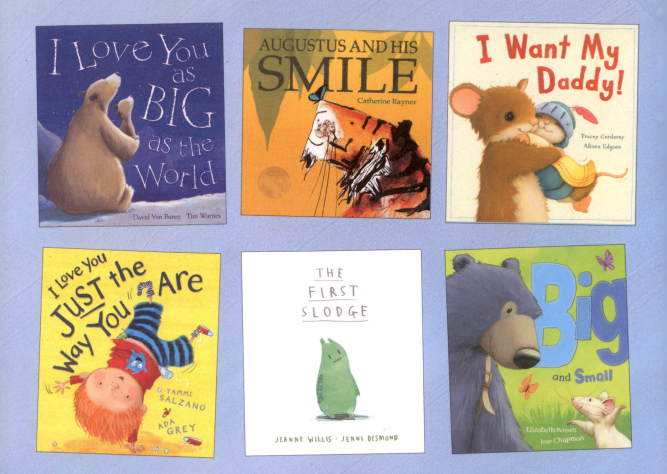

Heartwarming stories to treasure
from Little Tiger Press!

For information regarding any of the above titles
or for our catalogue, please contact us:
Little Tiger Press, 1 The Coda Centre,
189 Munster Road, London SW6 6AW
Tel: 020 7385 6333 E-mail: contact@littletiger.co.uk
www.littletiger.co.uk